JESUS ESCAPES FROM THE WICKED KING

ON THE first Christmas day, when the Baby Jesus was born, there was a very bad king named Herod living in a big palace nearby. God had put a bright new star in the sky when His Son Jesus was born. But the bad King Herod could not see it, even when he looked out the window. His heart was too wicked. God did not show His star to the bad King.

THE BAD King Herod heard some people talking. "God's Son has been born," the people said. "When He grows up He will be our king."

King Herod was *so* bad, he did not want God's Son around near him. He did not want Jesus to grow up and be king. "I'm the only king around here," he said.

Herod tried to find out where Jesus was, so he could kill the little Baby. What a wicked, mean old king Herod was!

WHERE IS that little King?" asked King Herod.

"We don't know exactly, but He's somewhere in Bethlehem," they told him.

Herod got so mad, he jumped up and down and yelled.

"All you soldiers, take your spears and swords. Go out and kill all the boy babies in Bethlehem. Kill *every one* of them. I'll have no little kings growing up around me!"

THE SOLDIERS started off in a big hurry, to do what Herod said. The King smiled to himself and rubbed his hands together. “Ah ha!” he said. “Baby Jesus will be killed this very day!”

But Herod was wrong. Something was happening in the dark night, and he knew nothing about it.

THE WICKED King Herod was sitting up late. He could not sleep because he was still so mad about the Child Jesus being born. Right outside his window an Angel was passing by, but he did not know it. The Angel was going to Bethlehem. The Angel woke Saint Joseph and whispered in his ear: "Hurry! Get up! Take the Child and His Mother and go to Egypt. Stay there until I tell you to come back."

SAINT JOSEPH got right up and called Mary. It was the middle of the night, and she was sound asleep. Most people do not like being told to get up in the middle of the night, but Mary did not fuss. She smiled and said, "I will do what God wants." She got right up.

MARY HAD to wake Baby Jesus, too, and get Him ready. She kissed Him and said, "Come, my little Lord Jesus! We are going for a long, long ride to Egypt. I will bundle You up so You won't get cold. We must hurry, hurry, hurry!"

Your next Treasure Box *will tell you what happened to the Holy Family in Egypt.*

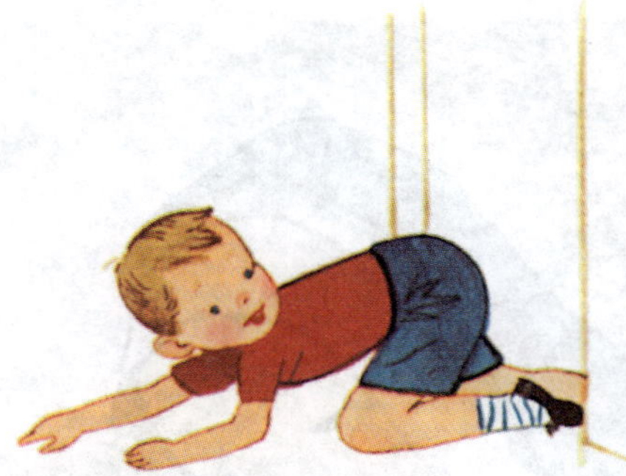

FANCY WALKS (Rebus)

I can walk like an  , shaking the floor,
I can sneak like a little  out through the door.
I can hop like a  and prance like a  .
I can jump like a  or a  on all fours.
I have fun when I walk like the things which I see,
And I almost forget that I'm actually ME.

THE RICH MAN'S RAGS

Once there was a rich man. He was very, very rich. Even his name was Mr. Rich.

When Mr. Rich was young, he had been very poor. But he tried to forget that. When he became rich he also forgot his mother and his old friends at home. They never heard from him again.

Mr. Rich thought only of himself. Everything he wanted he bought with his money.

One day he became very ill. Nobody came to see him. His new friends cared only about his money and his parties. They did not care that he was all alone now.

As Mr. Rich was lying there ill in his bed, something strange happened to him! Suddenly his room was filled with a bright light, and he saw someone standing by the door. The stranger's clothes were white as snow. His eyes seemed to look deep into Mr. Rich's soul.

"Who are you?" asked the sick man.

"I am the Angel of Death," answered the stranger. "I have been sent for you. Follow me."

The rich man was afraid. He did not want to leave his comfortable house and all the good things he owned.

"How did you get into my house?" he said. "I will call my servants and they will send you away."

The Angel smiled.

"My Master's word counts for more than yours," he said. "Follow me!"

"Give me time!" pleaded the rich man. "I have to look after my business. And you can see that I am not even dressed."

Again the Angel smiled.

"Your garment is waiting for you," he said. "Follow me."

He touched the sick man's eyes with his finger. All at once Mr. Rich found himself in a strange room. It was filled with hundreds and thousands of looms. On each loom a piece of fabric was being woven. But, although the looms were working, there seemed to be nobody in the room to look after them. Along the walls hung many garments made from the woven materials.

"Whose are those looms and gowns?" asked Mr. Rich. The Angel of Death answered: "They belong to the people on earth. All their deeds and thoughts are woven into a fabric. That fabric is made into the garment in which they will appear before the throne of God. Your garment is waiting for you."

Now the rich man looked again. He saw how different they all were. Some were rich and beautiful, fit for kings and queens. Others were simpler, but woven in a strong and regular pattern. Some were smoothly woven. Others looked ill-fitting and full of knots and holes.

There were more fabrics and garments in that one room than Mr. Rich had seen in all his life.

"Which one belongs to me?" he asked. He expected the

Angel to point to the scarlet robe with the gold-embroidery along the edges; or to the silk gown with the broad silver belt. For, after all, he was a rich man.

The Angel did not answer immediately. He looked at him as if he could read his thoughts.

"Where is my gown?" asked Mr. Rich impatiently. He was not used to being kept waiting. Now the Angel spoke.

"Here, my friend," he said, as he took a garment out of a dark corner and wrapped it around the rich man's shoulders.

"These miserable rags for me!" shouted Mr. Rich. His voice shook with fury. "Why, they are not good enough for a beggar to wear! Just look at all the holes and patches!"

"I know," answered the Angel. "But it is your gown. Remember: it was you who wove the material by the way you lived."

He pointed to the biggest tear.

"Do you remember your poor mother?" he asked gently. "These holes were made by you when you tore her out of your life."

For the first time in years the rich man thought of his mother. How she had worked for him when he was a child! How she had nursed him when he was sick! How she had shown him her love in so many ways! He felt that if she were with him now she would mend the tear in his garment, as she had mended his clothes when he was her little boy.

"I wish I could tell her that I love her," he murmured. "But now it is too late."

"Do you remember your friend who was in need and you would not help him?" the Angel asked. Again and again he asked the question: "Do you remember?" as he pointed to all the stains and holes and patches in the rich man's rags. Mr. Rich remembered all the selfish things he had done. He did not look proud any longer. He looked like a very sad and poor man.

"If only I could live my life again," he whispered, "how different it would be. If only I could make up for all the things I have done."

He began to weep bitterly. His tears rolled down his rags. But now a miracle happened! As they touched the fabric, each tear turned into a precious diamond. Soon the patches and stains were covered with the sparkling stones. The miserable rags shone with splendor.

The rich man did not notice it. He was still weeping.

"Oh, if only I could live again!" he sobbed.

"You are going to live, my friend," he heard a voice say. He thought it was the Angel of Death. But when he opened his eyes he saw the doctor standing by his bedside.

"Where am I? Am I not dead?" asked the rich man.

"You were close to death," said the doctor. "But the danger has passed. You will live."

"Thanks be to God!" exclaimed the patient, "that I have still time to mend my ragged garment!"

The doctor shook his head. He did not understand what the rich man was talking about. But Mr. Rich was too happy to care. He promised himself to do everything in his power to make up for the wrong he had done in his life.

His garment would be whole and beautiful when the Angel of Death called again to lead him before the Throne of God.

THE LAND OF

At evening when the lamp is lit,
Around the fire my parents sit;
They sit at home and talk and sing
And do not play at anything.

Now, with my little gun, I crawl
All in the dark along the wall,
And follow round the forest track
Away behind the sofa back.

There, in the night, where none can spy,
All in my hunter's camp I lie,
And play at books that I have read
Till it is time to go to bed.

STORY-BOOKS

These are the hills, these are the woods,
These are my starry solitudes;
And there the river by whose brink
The roaring lions come to drink.

I see the others far away
As if in firelit camp they lay,
And I, like to an Indian scout,
Around their party prowled about.

So, when my nurse comes in for me,
Home I return across the sea,
And go to bed with backward looks
At my dear land of Story-books.

—*Robert Louis Stevenson*

WHO COMES TO VISIT YOU? (a game)

This is a game that can be played inside or out-of-doors. All join hands and form a circle, in the center of which one of the players is sitting, his eyes blindfolded. The circle moves around him, chanting:

Our house is windowless,
there is no light to see.
If you drop in I'll have to guess:
"Who comes to visit me?"

At the word "me," all stop, and the child who now happens to stand behind the one in the center asks:

"Who comes to visit you?"

If the blindfolded child guesses right, the one who asked the question is "it." Otherwise the circle moves around again.

SUNNY GOES TO CATECHISM CLASS

Father George wanted all the children in the village of Matongu to know about God. So he set out to see all the fathers and mothers to tell them his plans. When he got to Sunny's hut, he saw Sunny's father, Bugomi, up on top of the hut, fixing the roof.

"Good morning, Bugomi," said Father George.

"Good morning, Father," said Bugomi as he climbed down to the ground.

"Bugomi," Father George said, "I think it's time John learned about God. Remember when he was a tiny baby and he almost died? And I cured him? Well, it was God and not I who cured him that day. I also poured water over his head and made him a child of God. So he really belongs to God. John must now start to learn about God."

Bugomi had heard about a god whose name was Leza, who created everything, but he understood that Leza could not be bothered about people, so why should people bother about him?

Father George said, "On the contrary, Bugomi, God not only created us all, but He takes good care of us all. Just as a loving father takes care of his family." And he told Bugomi that God even sent His Son to die for all of us.

Bugomi was interested, and he talked quite a long time to Father George. Finally, Father George got Bugomi to promise to come up to the chapel to hear more, and then he arranged to have Sunny John come for catechism lessons with the other children of the village.

Sunny was quite excited, but Wupsy was *thrilled* to think that his own special baby was going to learn about God. And *he* was going to help. Indeed he was!

The day he was to go to his first lesson, Ntaka-Ntaka dressed Sunny in his very best clothes and took him down to where all the children had gathered for their lesson, and left him there. Sunny didn't know very many of the children at first, but he soon found that the ones he talked to were very nice and might become very good friends later. Father Christopher, who was in charge, sat down on a stump of a tree and had all the children sit around him in a circle as he started his lesson. This is what he said:

"Once upon a time," he began, "God lived all by Himself in His own house which is called Heaven, and God was very happy. But God wanted to share this happiness. He couldn't do that because there wasn't anybody else, anywhere. God was all alone."

"But weren't there some people at Matongu?" asked one little boy.

"Not even at Matongu," Father Christopher told him. "There wasn't anyone else at all because there was nowhere for them to live. But God did very much want to make other people happy, so what do you think He did?"

"Maybe he made some other people?" somebody said.

"That's right," said the priest. "He made other people, and first of all He made some spirits called Angels who could live with Him at once in Heaven." The children looked frightened because they knew about bad spirits, so Father Christopher quickly explained, "These were good spirits, not like the *maleza* or the *mizimou*. Angels are beautiful spirits who serve God and help Him to do good to other people."

"So there were some other people?" asked another of the children.

"Not at once," replied Father Christopher. "But after the Angels, God thought about making some other people, not just spirits, but spirits with bodies as well, people like you and me. First of all, though, He had to make someplace for them to live, so He made the world and the sun and the moon and plants and animals."

"Yes, I know," said one of the older children, who had already been taught the traditions of the country. "He made a man called *Mkanakufwa* and a woman called *Kao* and a cow, and they all had seeds in their hair and *Leza* dropped them down from Heaven just like rain."

Father Christopher was very interested in this African legend, and he explained carefully: "It's true God made a man and a woman, but He didn't drop them down from Heaven because they might have been hurt if He had. He made them in a beautiful garden where there were lots of flowers and plants and corn and lots of animals, even cows, which were all friends together, and they were all very happy."

Sunny had been listening because he loved to listen to people tell stories and he thought Father Christopher told them better than anyone else in the whole of Matongu. After a while Sunny began thinking about cows and lions and especially the lion he heard just the night before, way in the middle of the forest. So Wupsy had to whisper in his ear to make him pay attention. Then he went on whispering to help Father Christopher explain to Sunny how much God loved all the people He had made. Of course, Wupsy did not use any words, Angels don't need to. But Sunny understood very well indeed.

And so the lesson went on, with Father Christopher explaining, and Wupsy and the other Guardian Angels busy helping. The children were very interested, and when they went home they told their fathers and mothers all that they had heard, and *they* were interested, too. Soon there was quite a crowd that went up to see Father George and Father Christopher. Bugomi and Ntaka-Ntaka were not the only parents that were interested. They were joined by lots of friends, and Father Christopher's classes became bigger and bigger.